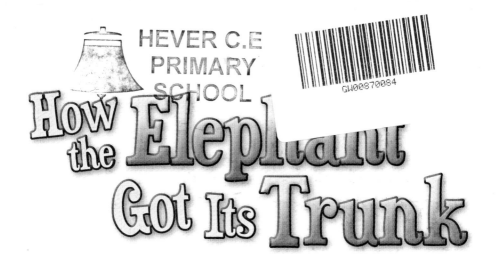

How the Elephant Got Its Trunk

by Alison Reynolds

illustrated by Alessia Trunfio

a Capstone company — publishers for children

Engage Literacy is published in the UK by Raintree.
Raintree is an imprint of Capstone Global Library Limited, a company incorporated in England and Wales having its registered office at 264 Banbury Road, Oxford, OX2 7DY – Registered company number: 6695582

www.raintree.co.uk

Illustration copyright © Capstone/Alessia Trunfio

Editorial credits
Gina Kammer, editor; Charmaine Whitman, designer; Katy LaVigne, production specialist

How the Elephant Got Its Trunk

ISBN: 978 1 4747 4708 0

Printed and bound in India.

Contents

Chapter 1
Elephant trouble

"Oops," said Nambo, tripping over a log.

His mother tumbled over as a boulder of a baby elephant crashed into her legs. "Please be careful, Nambo," she gasped.

Tears filled Nambo's eyes because he didn't mean to be clumsy, but he just was.

"Why am I so clumsy?"

"Because all baby elephants are," said his mother. "One day, when you are older, you will grow into your body. Take care until then or somebody might get hurt." She pressed her short, grey nose against his short nose.

Nambo snuggled into his mother, his stomach rumbling. "What's for lunch?" he asked.

"Some leaves that blew off the palm trees last night."

"But that was breakfast," grumbled Nambo.

He pointed to red flowers in the trees. "Can't we have those? They are delicious."

"If the breeze blows them down, we can," said his mother. "Elephants can't climb."

"I bet crocodiles don't eat boring palm leaves because they're always smiling. What do crocs eat for lunch?"

"Don't be silly, Nambo. I need to gather our food, so go on and play."

Nambo didn't think it was a silly question, but his mother's ears were flapping, which was a sign she was unhappy. Nambo sighed and walked towards the jungle. None of the other animals ever wanted to play with him. He always fell on top of them, pushed them over or asked too many questions. He took a deep breath. Today would be different. He would make a friend.

Chapter 2
A walk in the jungle

It got hotter as Nambo wandered deeper into the jungle, but nobody was around. Above a twig snapped, and Nambo spied a pair of golden eyes gazing at him through the leaves.

"Hello," said Nambo. "Your spots really hide you in the tree. Will you play, Leopard?"

Leopard shook his head. "My tail still hurts from when you stood on it last week."

"I'll be careful," promised Nambo.

"Sorry, it's lunch time." Leopard sprung down and slunk away.

"Wait," shouted Nambo. "Can you tell me what crocs eat for lunch?"

"Keep away from crocs, Nambo, because you don't want to know what they eat," shouted Leopard over his shoulder.

Nambo frowned. That was not true. He did want to know what crocs ate for lunch.

Nambo reached a blue pool in the very middle of the jungle. A pink feather lay next to a bush, so the little elephant pushed his way through the leaves.

"Are you hiding, Flamingo?" Nambo asked.

"I was looking for something," said Flamingo.

"For what?" asked Nambo.

"A bit of quiet away from noisy elephants," said Flamingo, fluffing his feathers.

"Are you pink because you have sunburn?" asked Nambo.

"No," said Flamingo. "The food I eat makes me pink."

"Are you blushing because you have such a long bendy neck?"

"I love my neck. Look what I can do." The flamingo twisted his long neck into the shape of a question mark.

Nambo stumbled forward to take a closer look and stepped on the bird's foot.

"Oops! Sorry."

"Ouch, my poor foot!" Flamingo limped away.

"Please, don't leave," cried Nambo.

"It's lunch time anyway," said Flamingo.

"But can you tell me what a croc has for lunch?"

Flamingo stopped. "Keep away from crocs," he said.

"Why?" asked Nambo.

"You don't need to know why," he replied.

Nambo watched Flamingo disappear. It really upset Nambo when the animals told him not to do something but would not explain why.

Chapter 3
Look before leaping

The pool sparkled in the sun and looked just right for a swim. "Yippee!" shouted Nambo as he leaped into the cool, clear water.

"Ouch!" growled a voice. "Haven't you heard of looking before you leap? You are so clumsy!" grumbled Hippo.

"I didn't know you were there," said Nambo. "Why does it seem like everybody is hiding from me?"

"Because wherever you go, somebody gets hurt. You can be such a bumbling baby elephant."

Nambo wasn't sure what that meant, but he knew he didn't like it. "I am not."

Hippo dragged herself out of the water. "I'm going to the river to get some peace and have lunch," she said.

Nambo watched Hippo waddle away. "Wait," he shouted. "Do you know what a crocodile has for lunch?"

"Why don't you ask one, Nambo?" growled Hippo. Nambo decided he would, so he headed towards the river.

Chapter 4
Crocodile River

Nambo charged through vines and tramped over logs. He knelt down to chew juicy green grass, and a twig jabbed his knee. Nambo held back tears and kept going.

Finally, he reached the river, and something squawked behind him. Nambo turned around and saw Flamingo.

"Hey," said Flamingo. "You're not really going to ask a croc what it has for lunch, are you?"

A croc's head popped up from the river. "Looking for me?"

"I want to ask what you eat for lunch," said Nambo.

Croc shook his head. "I can't hear you, young elephant. Come closer."

Nambo walked to the river's edge. "Don't go," whispered Flamingo.

The croc pleaded, "You're too far away. Come closer, please."

"Come back, Nambo," moaned Flamingo, flapping his wings.

Nambo splashed into the river. "What do you eat for lunch?" he shouted.

"You!" The croc flung his jaws wide open.

Chapter 5
Hippo in trouble

"Run!" shouted Flamingo. Nambo ran as fast as he could, his heart thumping. "I won't tell you I told you so, but I did," puffed Flamingo.

Finally, Nambo stopped and rested with Flamingo next to him. "I'll never talk to Hippo again after she told me to ask Croc what he has for lunch."

"Help!" shouted a voice. Hippo stood in the river.

"Croc nearly gobbled me up because of you," said Nambo. "I don't want to talk to you anymore so goodbye!"

"Wait," called Hippo. "I'm trapped between rocks, and water from the tide is coming in. If you don't help me, I'll drown."

Nambo said, "You can't trick me."

"I can't breathe underwater like a fish. Please help me," begged Hippo. The water reached Hippo's shoulders.

"You want lunch, and I think your lunch is me. I'm not going to be your food!" replied Nambo.

"I only eat plants," shouted Hippo. "I like water reeds, not tough elephant."

Chapter 6
The rescue mission

Nambo splashed out into the river towards Hippo. He pushed Hippo, but she didn't move. "Take my nose, and I'll pull you out that way."

Hippo grabbed onto Nambo's rubbery nose. The little elephant pulled and pulled. Hippo moved, then stopped.

"I can't do it by myself," said Nambo. "Flamingo, fly for help."

Nambo pulled a hollow reed at the water's edge. "Hippo, breathe through this reed like a snorkel if the water covers your head." Hippo gulped but held the reed tightly in her mouth like a straw.

Leopard padded into the water and grabbed Nambo's tail. They pulled and pulled so much that they fell over with a giant splash. The water started to cover Hippo.

"We'll tie ourselves to trees by the shore so we don't fall over," said Nambo. "Flamingo, help."

Flamingo wrapped his neck around a tree and gripped Leopard with his legs. Leopard pulled Nambo's tail. Hippo held Nambo's nose as tightly as she could.

Together, they pulled and tugged. Just as the water completely covered her, out popped Hippo. "Thank you!" cried Hippo.

Nambo smiled until he saw his image in the water. He jerked his head back, and a long trunk flapped up from where his nose once was.

Chapter 7
Trunks are the best

Nambo jumped back from his image in the water. "I'm so ugly!" shouted Nambo in distress. His shouts were so loud, all the jungle animals rushed out. His mother ran towards her son.

Giraffe bent down to Nambo. "You've got yourself a long nose there."

Nambo cried and cried. "Why did this happen? Why?" he cried.

For once, none of the animals groaned or grumbled when Nambo asked them why. They all looked with sad eyes at the little elephant.

"You're still Nambo," said his mother. "Come home, have a nap, have something to eat and you'll feel better."

Nambo was hungry, and without thinking, he used his long trunk to pick up some juicy grass. He chewed it slowly.

"No more kneeling and hurting your knees," said Flamingo.

Nambo dried his eyes with his trunk. He looked up and saw his favourite red flowers. With his long trunk, he plucked them off the tree and passed them to his mother. She smiled.

"It's great reaching tall things," said Giraffe.

Meanwhile, Nambo's mother and all the other elephants whispered together before hurrying towards Hippo. "Can you pull our noses? We want trunks, too."

"If Nambo wants me to," said Hippo. "Because of me you nearly lost your life, Nambo, yet you saved mine. Thank you."

Nambo grinned. "Here is one more thing my trunk can do." He aimed at Hippo.

SWISH!

The dripping hippo said, "I was hot after all that pulling! You are a good friend."

"The best friend anybody could have," said Flamingo.

Nambo smiled. He had friends, red flowers to eat and he knew what crocs ate for lunch.